This book belongs to:

_____

For Ben, Simon and Phoebe—E.D.
For Lil, my fellow star traveller—J.L.

OXFORD
UNIVERSITY PRESS

Great Clarendon Street, Oxford OX2 6DP

Oxford University Press is a department of the University of Oxford.
It furthers the University's objective of excellence in research, scholarship,
and education by publishing worldwide. Oxford is a registered trade mark of
Oxford University Press in the UK and in certain other countries

Text copyright © Ella Denton 2016
Illustrations copyright © Jamie Littler 2016

The moral rights of the author and artist have been asserted

Database right Oxford University Press (maker)

First published 2016

British Library Cataloguing in Publication Data available

Data available

ISBN: 978-0-19-9273940-7 (paperback)
ISBN: 978-0-19-273941-4 (eBook)

2 4 6 8 10 9 7 5 3 1

Printed in China

Paper used in the production of this book is a natural,
recyclable product made from wood grown in sustainable forests.
The manufacturing process conforms to the environmental
regulations of the country of origin.

INTERGALACTIC ED
and the SPACE PIRATES

ELLA DENTON
JAMIE LITTLER

OXFORD
UNIVERSITY PRESS

All seemed peaceful
and calm in outer space—
until Ed spotted something
strange through
his telescope . . .

'Cosmic calamity!'
said Ed to his cat, Sputnik.
'Something's wrong with the moon!'

Luckily, Ed knew just what to do.
He grabbed his backpack . . .

his Turbo Torch . . .

and Sputnik—Space Cat Extraordinaire.

Then he pushed a small book on his shelf sideways.
There was a whirring sound followed by a loud click—
and a hidden panel in Ed's bedroom wall slowly slid open.

Beyond it was . . .

Ed's Intergalactic Operations Headquarters!

Ed and Sputnik were ready for an Intergalactic Adventure!

They stepped into the
Space Transporter Capsule and

ZOOMED into space.

Suddenly, they spotted a ship.
But not just any ship . . .

The Interplanetary Plunderer was the **BIGGEST** pirate spaceship in the galaxy!

Ed landed just as a gang of pirates strode on deck.

'Quick! Hide!' he whispered, as the pirates began to sing.

Oooh! Arggh! Heave-ho!

Pull in the nets and off we go!

The pirates gave a **MIGHTY** heave and suddenly Ed couldn't believe his eyes.

'You can't tell us what to do, space flea!' said the captain.

'This moon is the SHINIEST
treasure we've ever seen!
And we WANTS IT!'

'But, er, the thing is the moon isn't actually shiny . . .' said Ed.

'What are you talking about, boy?' shrieked the captain. 'Just look at it!'

Ed picked up a cannonball and pointed his Turbo Torch at it.

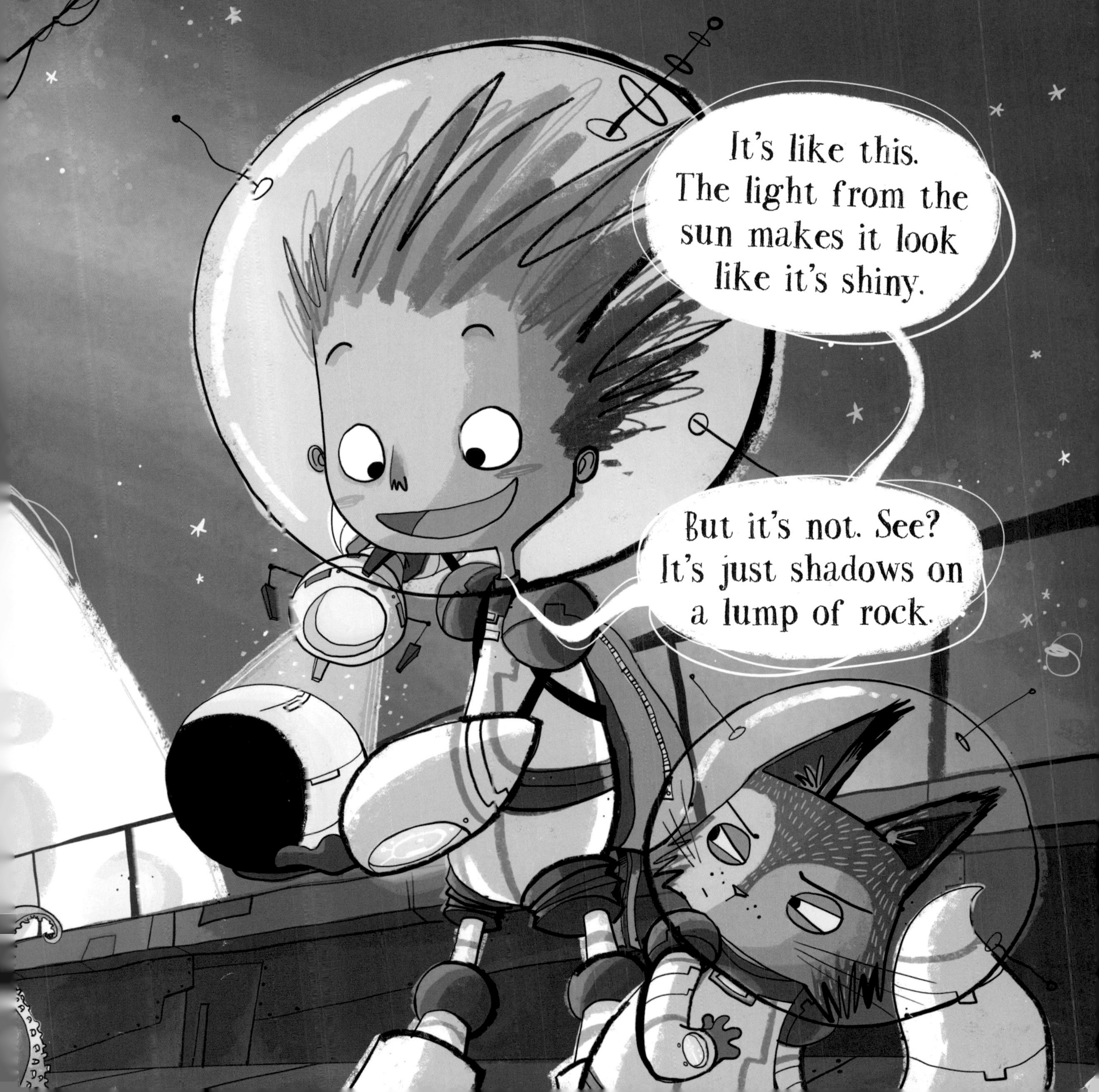

'All right, all right!' cried the captain. 'Have it your way! At least it's still the **BIGGEST** moon in the solar system.'

GANYMEDE

MERCURY

JUPITER

'But it's not, you see,' **said Ed.** 'Jupiter's moon Ganymede is . . .

'It's even bigger than the planet Mercury!'

This was the final straw.

'This little space flea thinks
he knows better than me!'
the captain shouted.

What should we
do about THAT,
eh, lads?

SPUTNIK!

Ed called, as he teetered on the edge of the plank.

HELP!

Suddenly, Sputnik thought of something.

He skittered across the deck and switched on the Turbo Torch.

Sputnik aimed its great beam of light upwards and then clambered up the mast.

With the pirate's chants sounding louder, he started to dance behind the sails.

'This is no time for mucking about!' yelled Ed.

But Sputnik had a clever idea . . .

As the light from the torch glowed in the sky, Sputnik's dance became the most magnificent shadow show the pirates had ever seen.

'Oooooooohh . . .' said the crew, totally transfixed.

The pirates sprang into action, scrambling up and down the rigging,

and all over the ship, trying to catch Sputnik,

all by the light
of the moon.

Well, by the
light of the
torch, in fact.

Because as the pirates
were trying to capture
the dancing cat, Ed had
secretly untied the net
and set the moon free.

The pirates hadn't even noticed and
now the moon was light years away.

'What a clever cat,' said Ed,
as Sputnik skipped over the
pirates and into his arms.

They leapt into the Space
Transporter Capsule and . . .

ZOOMED into space.

Soon they landed back on Earth.

Phew!

'That was close,' said Ed,
collapsing on the bed.

And all was peaceful and calm
in outer space once more.

Well, almost . . .